The Adventures of

Jules & Gertie

Esther Pearl Watson

HARCOURT BRACE & COMPANY

San Diego   New York   London

Requests for permission to make copies of any part of the work
should be mailed to: Permissions Department, Harcourt Brace & Company,
6277 Sea Harbor Drive, Orlando, Florida 32887-6777.

Library of Congress Cataloging-in-Publication Data
Watson, Esther Pearl.
The adventures of Jules & Gertie/Esther Pearl Watson.
p.   cm.
Summary: Cowgirl Jules and her multitalented horse, Gertie,
save the town folks from Mean Bulldog Pike and his rotten horse, Bullet.
ISBN 0-15-201975-8
[1. West (U.S.)—Fiction.   2. Humorous stories.]   I. Title.
PZ7.W3267Ag   1999
[E]—dc21   98-22267

First edition
A C E F D B

Printed in Singapore

The illustrations in this book were done in acrylics.
The display type was hand lettered by Esther Pearl Watson.
The text type was set in Memphis Medium.
Color separations by United Graphic Pte. Ltd., Singapore
Printed and bound by Tien Wah Press, Singapore
This book was printed on totally chlorine-free Nymolla Matte Art paper.
Production supervision by Stanley Redfern and Pascha Gerlinger
Designed by Linda Lockowitz

For my heroes
Granny and
Grandad

Out in the scratchy and blistery West
lived two sneaky weeds, Mean Bulldog
Pike and Bullet, his skunk of a horse.
Together they were sour as buttermilk,
rusty as nails, and the greediest outlaws
on the Western plains. Shoot, they would
even pry a dollar from a rattlesnake!

Pike and Bullet's latest scheme was a rotten old sideshow.
Those two lazy villains packed the town folks in a tent like
pickles and made them pay to watch Little Horn dance on
hot coals. That little buffalo had to go gallyfootin' this way
and that just to keep from being barbecued.

Just when Little Horn and the dusty folk felt that all hope was hog-tied, a cowgirl rode into town: a red bull's-eye named Jules. Genuine like leather. Strong like licorice.

Her horse, Gertie, could sing, dance, cook, make a mean cup of coffee, multiply, divide, and speak three languages.

Those brave gals tore through that tent like a hailstorm and broke Little Horn free.

Tough as hide, Jules lassoed Pike's knees and swung him round.
Gertie took the money bags and pitched them high.

Pike and Bullet bolted, kicking up a dust storm as they ran out
of town.

Under raining coins, Jules punched out a laugh, loud and true. Gertie sang a fiesta ditty and danced a victory jig. A Mexican twist. A blur of hide and hooves. Yikki yea!

From a ridge high above, Mean Bulldog Pike and his weasel
of a horse caught their breath and watched, jealous as snakes.
Foul ideas swam inside their swampy brains. They weren't
going to let a cowgirl and her horse make fools of them.

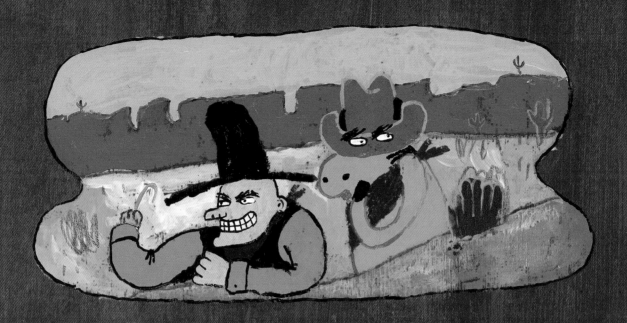

Then those two scoundrels had a sneaky idea. Gertie's singing and dancing could be turned into the biggest gold-grubbing sideshow around! So they began to think of ways to get rid of that smart-aleck hero and kidnap her fancy-pants show pony. Ways more crooked than corkscrews…

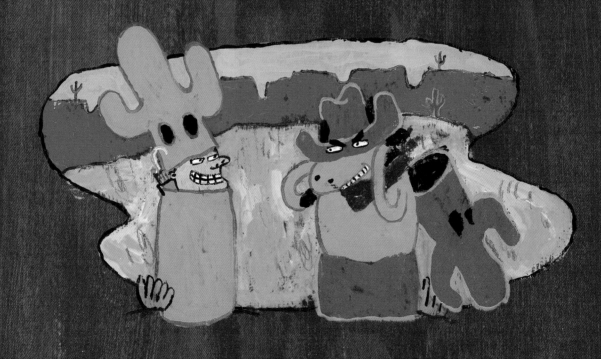

Down in the valley, Jules and Gertie wiped Little Horn's tears and cooled the heat from his hooves. Then they sent him home, laughing and singing Gertie's alphabet song.

Suddenly, Pike busted out of a cactus! He grabbed
Jules and held on straightjacket tight.

Mean Bulldog Pike laughed in her eye and said he'd throw her off the cliff to see if cowgirls could fly.

Jules knew Gertie would save her.
She would give Pike some of her

Very bad medicine!

But poor Gertie didn't have a chance. Bullet stuffed her into a feed sack quicker than a wink.

Then Pike carried Jules up the highest summit of Shide Poke Pass and threw her over the cliff's edge!

With Gertie the moneymaker in their bag, those sorry outlaws
rode off burnt on the bottom and soggy in the middle.
No one could stop them now!

But that wasn't the end of this cowgirl. Somehow, she would shuffle out of this spine-snapping spot and get her buddy back!

Meanwhile, Bulldog Pike and Bullet collected folks' gold all afternoon. People came from miles around to see Gertie perform her alphabet dances and multiplication songs.

Little Horn pulled back the curtains, and Gertie began to sing.
She felt lonely as an echo. Her best friend was gone, and those
greasy outlaws would drop her into a pit of squirming rattlers
if she stopped dancing.

Pike and Bullet spit and slobbered all over themselves with
excitement. They would be filthy rich at last!

Right then came the rumbling sound
of an earthquake…

and Jules thundered in on a longhorn cyclone!

In the middle of that big tumbleweed mess, Jules threw a loop round Gertie just before she dropped into that angry pit!

Between all those flying hats and horns, Pike
slipped off with a wheelbarrow full of money
and left his sidekick squealing behind.

Gertie roped that no-good horse
and left him crying on a cactus.

Just when Pike thought he had gotten away, Jules, brave and strong, popped him out of that wheelbarrow like popcorn on a hot skillet.

Gertie finished him off with some of her

Very bad medicine!

Scratchy Pike and his blistery horse were left with nothing but each other in the cold county jail. Little Horn and the town folks hooted, hollered, and threw their hooves and hats in the air.

Jules and Gertie were surely the best thing on the Western plains since biscuits and gravy: ten-gallon heroes with red bull's-eye talent.

As the sun set, Jules and Gertie rounded
up the day singing a fiesta ditty and
dancing a victory jig. A Mexican twist.
A blur of hooves and boots. And the West
was soothed like cinnamon. Yikki yea!

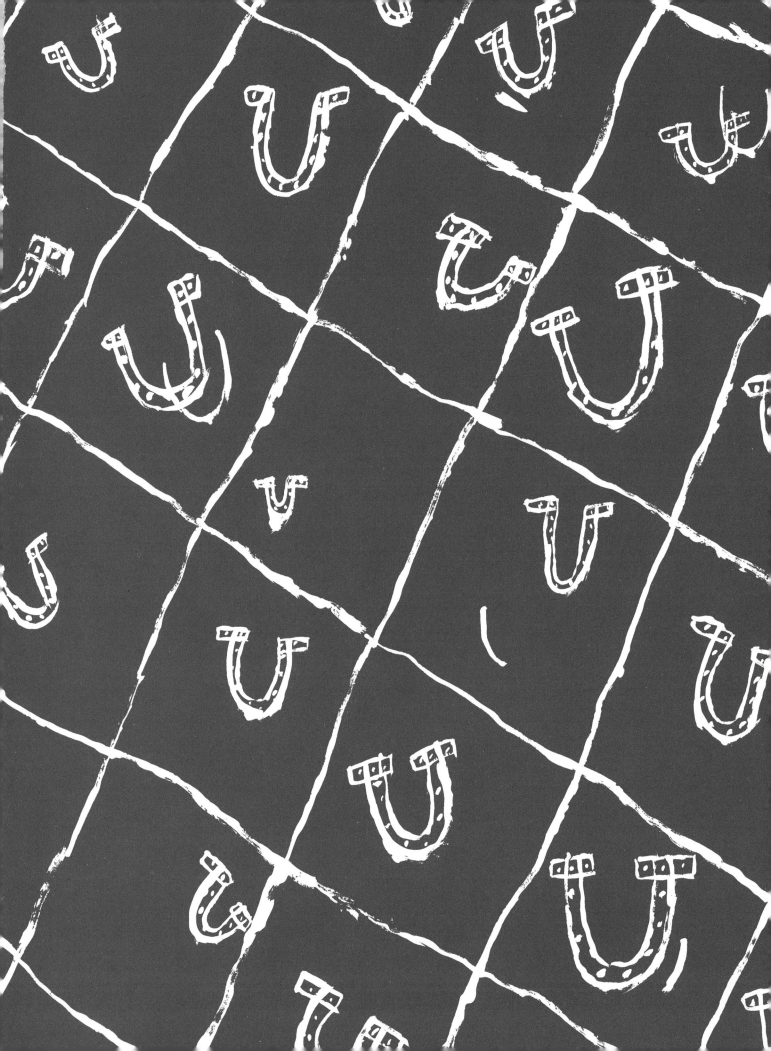